D1265997

They Call Me Mix
Me llaman Maestre

Written by: Lourdes Rivas

Edited in Spanish by: Alicia Arellano

Illustrated by: Breena Nuñez

Designed by: Caro Reyes

Library of Congress Control Number: 2018913385
ISBN: 978-0-692-14883-9 (hardcover)

Short Stack Font by James Grieshaber used in this book is
licensed under the SIL Open Font License, Version 1.1.

For permissions, bulk orders, or if you receive defective
or misprinted books, please email maestrxlourdes@gmail.com.
For book-related updates, follow @theycallmemix on Instagram.

Dedicated to every student I've ever worked with, from Lynwood to San Francisco to Boyle Heights to Oakland to Berkeley.

Dedicado a cada estudiante con quien he trabajado, de Lynwood a San Francisco a Boyle Heights a Oakland a Berkeley.

 ♡ ♡ Made with love in Oakland, California ♡ ♡

Are you
a boy or a girl?

How can
you be both?

¿Eres
niño o niña?

¿Cómo puedes
ser de los dos?

Some days I am both.

Some days I am neither.

Most days, I am everything in between.

Algunos días soy de los dos.

Algunos días soy ninguno.

La mayor parte del tiempo, soy todo entre los dos.

Before I was born, my mom had two different names ready for me: Daniel and Lourdes.

I would be Daniel, like my tío, if they decided I was a boy and Lourdes, like my tía, if they decided I was a girl. Both names come from my mom's siblings in México.

Antes de que yo naciera, mi mamá tenía dos nombres listos para mí: Daniel y Lourdes.

Sería Daniel como mi tío si ellos decidieran que yo era niño y sería Lourdes como mi tía si ellos decidieran que yo era niña. Los dos nombres vienen de la familia de mi mamá en México.

When I was born, everyone decided and agreed
that I was a girl,
so they named me Lourdes.

*Cuando yo nací, todos decidieron y se pusieron
de acuerdo que yo era niña,
entonces me nombraron Lourdes.*

As a kid, I never felt like *just* a girl. I never felt right knowing everyone was deciding and agreeing that I was a girl.

De pequeñ@ nunca me sentía como *solo* una niña. Nunca me sentí bien sabiendo que todos decidieron y se pusieron de acuerdo que yo era niña.

I also didnt feel like *just* a boy. I knew in my heart that I could never choose one or the other.

I knew in my heart that I wanted to be free every day to just be me, without thinking about choosing only girl or only boy.

Tampoco me sentía como *solo* un niño. Sentía en mi corazón que nunca podría escoger solo uno.

Sentía en mi corazón que quería ser libre cada día sin tener que escoger solo niña o solo niño.

I always felt like a little of both.

I wanted people to believe me.

I wanted people to celebrate me.

Siempre me sentía como una mezcla de los dos.

Quería que todos me creyeran.

Quería que todos me celebraran.

I imagined myself like a book. My outside cover told only one part of my story. Inside, I was bursting with imagination.

Me imaginaba como un libro. Mi portada contaba sólo parte de mi historia. Adentro, yo tenía demasiada imaginación.

Even though I knew this, I still didn't know how to explain it to anyone else but myself, so I went on agreeing with what others called me.

Aunque sabía todo esto, no sabía cómo explicárselo a alguien más entonces seguí pretendiendo que estaba de acuerdo con los demás.

Agreeing with others was like ignoring my heart. Ignoring your heart makes everything *very* difficult.

Pretendiendo es como ignorar a tu corazón. Ignorar tu corazón hace todo *muy* difícil.

You should never ignore your heart.

Nunca deberías ignorar tu corazón.

Have you ever noticed how almost everything is divided into Boys and Girls?

People create categories because they think it makes life easier. This kind of thinking is binary.
It's either one or the other.

¿Has notado que casi todo en el mundo está dividido entre Niños y Niñas?

La gente crea categorías porque piensan que hace todo más fácil. Este tipo de pensar es binario. Es uno o el otro.

But when it comes
to people, especially
people like me, gender
categories like BOY and GIRL
make so many things difficult.

What should I do?

Where do I fit in?

Where *can* I fit in?

Pero cuando estamos hablando de personas, especialmente de personas como yo, las categorias NIÑO y NIÑA dificultan tantas cosas.

¿Dónde *puedo* caber?

¿Dónde quepo yo?

¿Qué debería hacer yo?

HERE! We are transgender. We are not one or the other. We flow free like water in a river. We are non-binary. We're not *just* girls. We're not *just* boys.

We're both and everything in between. Everything makes sense! I understand more of who I am. I can share how I feel now!

¡AQUÍ! Somos transgénero. Nuestro género no es uno ni el otro. Fluye libre como agua en un río. Es no-binario. No somos *solo* niñas. No somos *solo* niños.

Somos de los dos y de todo entre los dos. ¡Todo tiene sentido! Ahora entiendo más de quien soy yo. ¡Ahora sí puedo compartir como me siento!

THIS IS YOUR COMMUNITY

I learned it's okay to disagree with everyone who looks at me and says I am a girl. It's okay to say,

"I'm not just a girl or just a boy.
I'm both and everything in between.
Instead of <u>she</u>, you can just say my name or use <u>they</u>."

Go ahead, try it!

Aprendí que está bien estar en desacuerdo con todos los que me ven y dicen que soy niña.

Está bien decir:

—No soy solo una nina ni solo un niño.
Soy de los dos y todo entre los dos.
En vez de <u>ella</u>, puedes decir mi nombre o usar <u>elle</u>.

¡Dale, inténtalo!

Many people understand that my gender is something for only me to decide. They ask what I'd like to be called. They learn to use non-binary words for me like <u>they</u> or just my name. They support me.

Muchas personas entienden que mi género es mi propia decisión. Me preguntan cómo me gustaría que me llamen. Aprenden a usar palabras no-binarias para mí, como <u>elle</u> o solo mi nombre. Me apoyan.

And some people cannot understand how it is possible for me to disagree with them and decide on my own gender.

Otras personas no entienden cómo es posible que yo esté en desacuerdo con ellos sobre mi propio género.

They continue saying I am a girl. They continue using the pronoun <u>she</u> for me.

Sometimes they even use hurtful words towards me. They disregard how I feel and what I need.

Continúan diciendo que soy niña. Continúan usando el pronombre <u>ella</u> para mi.

Algunas veces hasta usan palabras para lastimarme. Ignoran cómo me siento y lo que necesito.

I stay away and try to ignore them.

I stay away and try to remember that they have some learning to do.

I stay away and try not to let it bother me too much.

Me alejo e intento ignorarlos.

Me alejo e intento recordar que ellos tienen mucho que aprender.

Me alejo y no dejo que eso me moleste tanto.

Thankfully, I met and made friends with other smart, talented, and beautiful non-binary people.

Lo mejor de todo es que encontré amig@s inteligentes, talentos@s, hermos@s, y no-binarios.

We get together and do fun things like
have BBQs, play games,

Nos juntamos para hacer
carne asada, jugar juegos,

hacer fogatas,
acampar, andar en
bicicletas, mirar películas...

build bonfires,
go camping, go on
bike rides, watch movies...

make art, attend protests, create films, take pictures of each other, dance a lot, cook food together.

BLACK LIVES MATTER

hacer arte, participar en protestas, crear películas, tomarnos fotos, bailar mucho, cocinar juntos.

We listen to each other. We believe each other.
We celebrate each other!

Nos escuchamos. Nos creemos en nosotr@s mismos.
¡Nos celebramos!

I grew up and became a teacher.

I am a non-binary teacher.
I teach my students about respecting all genders.
We practice with each other.

Crecí y ahora soy maestre.

Les enseño a mis estudiantes
a respetar gente de todos los géneros.
Practicamos uno con el otro.

I teach my students that non-binary people look, dress and sound all kinds of different ways. I teach my students that it's okay to change and play with words to make them fit us. My students learn to call me Mx. Lourdes because I am a mix!

Les enseño a mis estudiantes que gente no-binaria
se ve, se viste, y se oyen de distintas formas.
Les enseño a mis estudiantes que algunas veces
necesitamos cambiar y jugar con palabras un poco
para que nos sirvan mejor. ¡Mis estudiantes aprenden
a llamarme maestre porque soy de los dos!

--F f --G g --H h --I i --J j --K k

And you too, can
decide for yourself.
If you ever feel in
your heart that you
don't agree with what
people say you are,
remember that there
are many of us out
there cheering you on.

Speak your truth!
Live your truth!

Y tú también puedes
decidir por ti mism@.
La gente siempre va a
pensar lo que piensa,
pero si en tu corazón
no estás de acuerdo con
lo que la gente diga de ti,
recuerda que somos
muchos en el mundo que
te apoyan y celebran.

¡Habla tu verdad!
¡Vive tu verdad!

Being transgender
is being free.

Ser transgénero
es ser libre.

Being transgender
is fearless.

Ser transgénero
es valiente.

Being transgender
is beautiful.

Ser transgénero
es lindo.

NOTE TO THE READER

For the past five years, I've been teaching Kindergarten. If you know anything about Kindergarteners, you know they're endlessly imaginative and curious about the world around them, and they soak up everything we teach them — whether implicitly or explicitly. I witness the strong (and very binary) ideas kids have around gender every day. They almost always ask "are you a boy or a girl?"

In no way is this a story about all transgender people. In no way is this a story about all non-binary people. This is simply my story. I wrote it out and pursued its publication so I can use it in my classroom to bring back imagination and possibility to the way kids approach and think about gender.

Pronouns can be as personal to someone as their name. One should never assume to know a person's pronoun, just like we don't go around assuming we know people's names. It's okay to ask. And if someone shares their pronouns with you, don't question them. Thank them for sharing and use those pronouns in the same way you would use their name after meeting. It's also okay to reimagine a whole new pronoun for yourself. Play with it and live your truth!

NOTA AL LECTOR

Por los últimos cinco años, he enseñado en un Jardín de Niños. Si sabes algo acerca de esa etapa, los niños de esa edad son inmensamente imaginativos y curiosos acerca del mundo que los rodea, y absorben todo lo que se les enseña, ya sea implícito o explícito. Frecuentemente he sido testigo de las ideas fuertes (y muy binarias) que tienen los niños alrededor del género. Ellos casi siempre me preguntan ¿"eres un chico o una chica"?

Esta historia, de ninguna manera es acerca de toda la gente transgénero. Así como, de ninguna manera es acerca de toda la gente no binaria. Esta, simplemente es mi historia. Yo la escribí y perseveré en su publicación para poder usarla en mi clase, y así regresar la imaginación y el enfoque que tienen los niños acerca del género.

Los pronombres, para alguien, pueden ser tan personales como su propio Nombre. Uno nunca debería asumir saber el pronombre de una persona, exactamente igual como no asumimos saber su Nombre. Esta bien preguntar. Si alguien comparte su pronombre, no lo cuestionamos. Agradécele por compartirlo y úsalo en la misma manera como usarías su Nombre después de conocerle. También está bien reinventar un nuevo pronombre para Tí mismo. ¡Juega con el y vive tu verdad!

LOURDES RIVAS BIO:

Lourdes was born and raised in Lynwood, CA. This is their first Children's Book. They currently live their non-binary life in the Bay Area, teaching Kindergarten.

BREENA NUÑEZ BIO:

Breena is a working cartoonist, musician & youth arts educator born into an immigrant family from El Salvador & Guatemala. The work she produces includes black & white illustrations that are influenced by her identity as a gender nonconforming Central American weirdo from the Bay Area. She previously studied at SFSU with a degree in Visual Communication Design & is currently studying at California College of the Arts to earn an MFA in Comics. She believes in the power of connecting struggles & marginalized narratives through zines & comic books.

BIO de LOURDES RIVAS:

Lourdes nació y creció en Lynwood, CA. Este es su primer libro infantil.

Lourdes es maestre de Kinder y vive su vida no-binaria en el Área de La Bahía de California.

BIO de BREENA NUÑEZ:

Breena es una caricaturista, música y educadora en artes juveniles, nacida dentro de una familia emigrante proveniente de El Salvador y Guatemala. El trabajo que ella produce incluye ilustraciones en blanco y negro influenciadas por su identidad como una coloquial Centroamericana del área de la Bahía. Breena previamente estudió en SFSU obteniendo una licenciatura en Diseño de Comunicación Visual, y actualmente estudia en el California College of the Arts para obtener una Maestría en Bellas Artes con especialidad en Comicidad. Ella cree mucho en el poder que tiene la conexión de las batallas y las narrativas marginadas a través de las revistas y los libros de caricaturas.

Thank you to all of the anonymous & non-anonymous Kickstarter backers!!!

Virginia Escobar, Alexander Bryn Penfield, Brook Pessin-Whedbee, Miriam Macías y Remigio Rivera, Niko "Torito" Hughes, Chicana Karla, Laura Rivas, Lizbeth Rivas, Nancy Angel, Ariana Gonzalez, Elisa Diana Huerta, Paceyn Julia O'Grady Specht, Cristal Esparza, Isabel Cooney-Ovalle, Christina Ung, Ava & Naomi, Lucero Lupercio Anguiano, Yvonne Tran, Amanda Pharis, David Valdez, A. Hua, mitoazul y ollín, Abby Taheri-Woodworth, Anastasia Gomes, Dyan, Lu Quetzalli, Cristian Gabriel F. Cruz, Dora P. Casetta, Dawn Stahura, Sandy Rodriguez (Lani's mama), Rachel Larson, Myra Garcia, Cati de los Rios, Carol Valdez, Maricruz Ceceña, Megan Pamela Ruth Madison, Julia Sen & Ravi Sen Campopiano, Sean E. Enloe, M.D., Brisa, Rocio Guzman, Emily Encina, Familia Arellano San Pedro, David Rodríguez, Maria Zamudio, Evans-Moyer family, Innosanto Nagara, Lourdes Mendoza, Jennifer Rodriguez, Leo & Abby, Sabrina Zarco, Mel Reyes & Sol Almuina, Lilac Vylette Maldonado, Melinda James, Mayra Gonzalez, Amanda Abarbanel, Alma López, Kristina Veasley, Anonymous, Venus Mulan, Lisa Kelly, Estelle Davis, Berenice Dimas, Anna Liisa Moter, Lani Rodriguez, Maria, Ashley Haden-Peaches, Josephine Pham, Jenna T. Baughman, Angelica, Roe Allen, Bere & Arnetta Villela-Smith, Mahfam Malek, M. Sheffrin, Tallulah Mae, Cora & Marlo Saloner, Kristen & Ziona Brock-Petroshius, Moira Farrell, Isis Piccillo, Hannah Yiu, Jason Martens, Yessica Frias, Robin Bogoshian, Christine Mcquaid, Bren, Fiona Schultz, Dana Blanchard, Green A.C., Carrie, Michelle Valente, Sasha, Kristen, Heba & Nayeli, Aeryca Steinbauer, Farima Pour-Khorshid, Mitali Purkayastha, J. Lor, Mx. Collier, Kay Cuajunco, Patricia Riestra, Atalanta Sungurov, Shadia Fayne Wood, Christine Irvine, Eduardo Muñoz-Maceira, Elena Martin, Sophia Simon-Ortiz, Gaba, Christian Castro, Neda Said, Raul Hernandez, Liza Lutzker, Ashley Barajas Montano, Team J, Joshua Logan May, Carol Umanzor, J. Little, Abi Colbert-Sangree, Mika Cade, Stephanie Markham, Stephanie, Micah Tasaka, Sukaina Farrukh, J. Varko, Gabriela Padilla, Emelia, Amanda McAllister-Wallner, Avery WK, Kelsey Mac, Thea Quiray Tagle, zizi bandera, Adrian Uliasz, Dulce Soledad Ibarra, Ilana Guckenheimer, Alicia Doktor, Theresa Madaus, Jess, Magz FC, SG Gettman, Mydiem & Lital, Sarah Ann Nelson, Natii, Lisa Jordan, Hannah TerBeek, Rosalyn Lam, Noam Zackon, B Cavello, Elliot Harper, Candy, Adrian Uliasz, Alessa B, Pi Kelly, Araceli Leon, Mejia-Quezada family, Sana Teramoto, Janet Mejia, Lupita Rivas Kramer, Heather Merrill, Daniel Shedd, Emily Teixeira, Sully Ross, Ivonne Ortega, Jennifer Pineda, Nguyen Louie, Team O from Seattle, Kim Westheimer, Smith-Gonzalez Family, Melissa Kim, Lore, Camila Vivanco Murphy, Robert Liu-Trujillo, Amber M., Sarae Pacetta, Thi Bui, Sarah Guerra, Gr Keer, Jenn LR Hernandez, Alma Rubio, Aly, Maia, Kobabe, Maureen L. Hartman, A + A Developers, Laurin Mayeno, Jaden Love, Alice Vasquez, Dr. T, Sine Hwang Jensen, Windy Sanchez, Jennifer Galindo, Ramses Rodstein, Tyler Cohen, Cynthia Enciso, Cindy D. Umanzor, Rachel Concitis, Leslie Palacios-Helgeson, Nessa Mahmoudi, Lisette Arellano-Avalos, Laura/Remus Short, Julie Phillips, Jill Contreras, Susan Roscigno, David Wang, Charlie McNabb, Brian, Sarah & Joshua Williams, Oregon Lesbian Feminist, Basty, Estella Sisneros, Laura C. Morales, Sharon McKellar, Judy Walgren, Mx. Lupe Blanco, Mx. Gorrin, Constantinos Antzakas, Cara Jaclyn M., Lo Bénichou, Tara Malik, Rachel May, Lauren W., Austin Dougherty, Leo Orleans, Amy Martin, Abe & Estrella Saldana, YaVette Holts, Adilia Torres, Eric Barbus, Tessa Lauren, Angela López & Milo Sánchez

CPSIA information can be obtained
at www.ICGtesting.com
Printed in the USA
LVHW072123241119
638366LV00018B/177/P